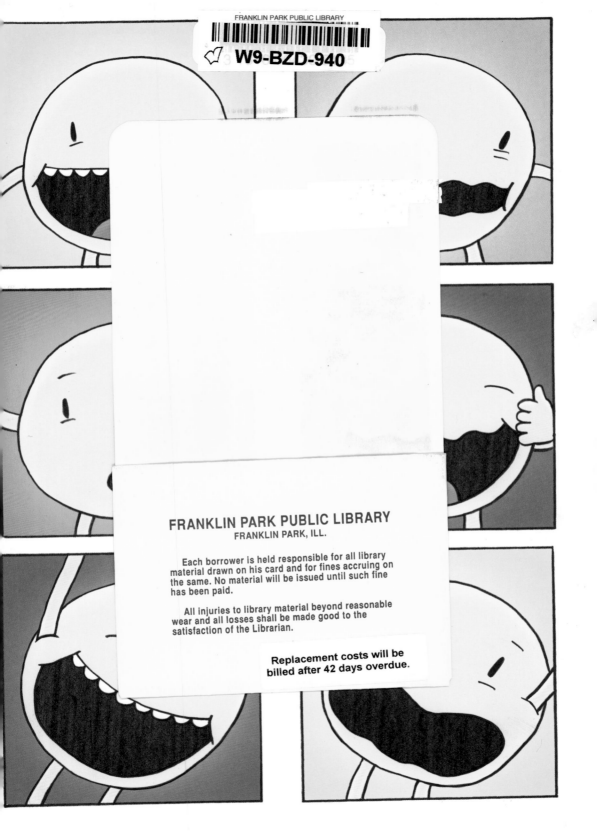

To Noah—M.T.

A **Jump•into•Chapters** Book

Copyright © 2014 Michael Townsend
All rights reserved/CIP data is available.
Published in the United States 2014 by
Blue Apple Books, 515 Valley Street,
Maplewood, NJ 07040
www.blueapplebooks.com
First Edition 02/14
Printed in China
ISBN: 978-1-60905-365-9

2 4 6 8 10 9 7 5 3 1

J-GN
MR. BALL
430-5135

MR. BALL MAKES A TO-DO LIST

Michael Townsend

FRANKLIN PARK LIBRARY
FRANKLIN PARK, IL
BLUE APPLE

BUT HE DOES HAVE A  pet cat!

HER NAME IS Ms. Kitty Cow. MOO-OW!

MR. BALL LOVES HIS CAT AND HIS FRIENDS!

PLUS, HE LOVES making TO-DO lists!

PART 1.

Mr. Ball And His To-Do Lists

Mr. Ball loves To-do lists!

Here is one of his lists

See Mr. Ball start that list!

See Mr. Ball chase an ice cream truck.

See Mr. Ball start to build Kitty a house!

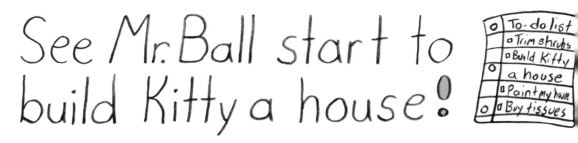

To-do list
☐ Trim shrubs
☐ Build Kitty
   a house
☐ Paint my house
☐ Buy tissues

See Mr. Ball **NOT** finish...

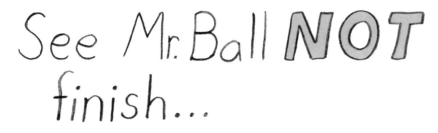

See Mr. Ball climb and paint...

To-do list
☐ Trim shrubs
☐ Build Kitty a house
☐ Paint my house
☐ Buy tissues

See Mr. Ball fall...

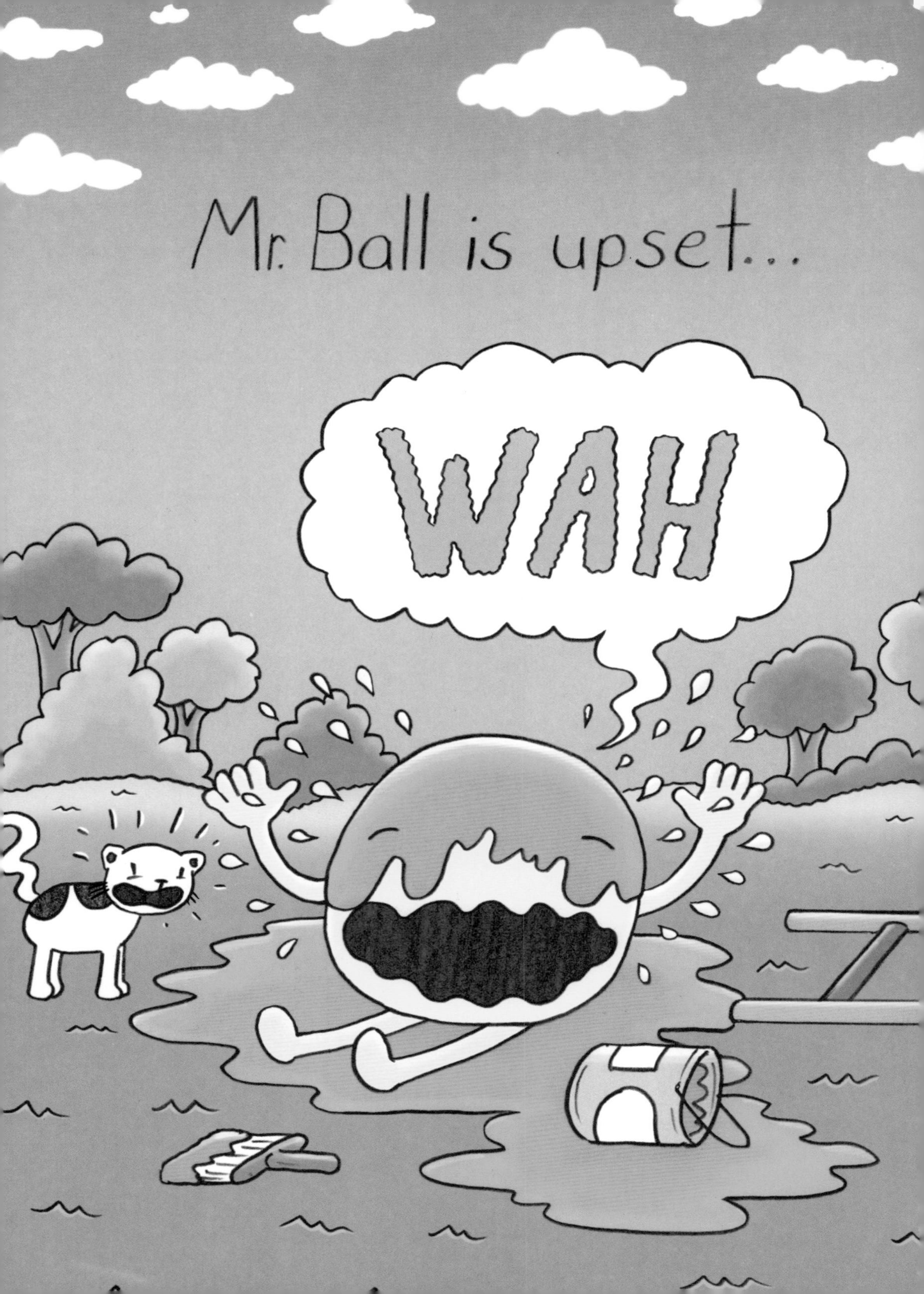
Mr. Ball is upset...
WAH

Mr. Ball needs a tissue...
but...

Mr. Ball needs to work on finishing the things he has started.

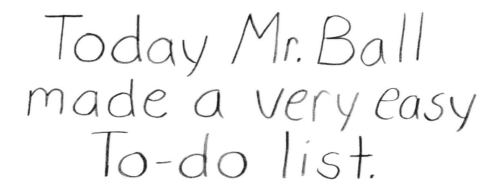

Today Mr. Ball made a very easy To-do list.

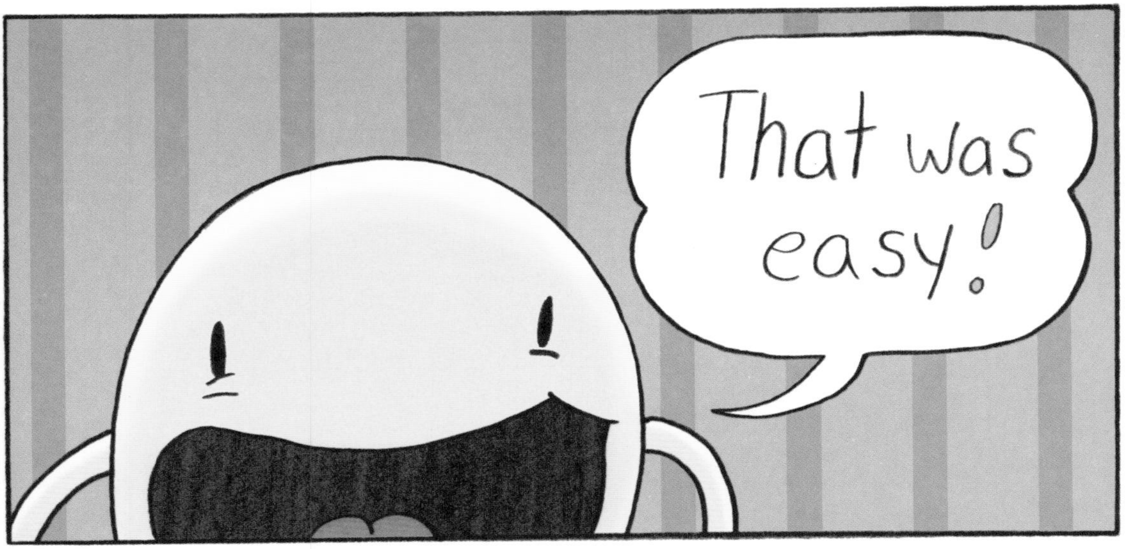
That was easy!

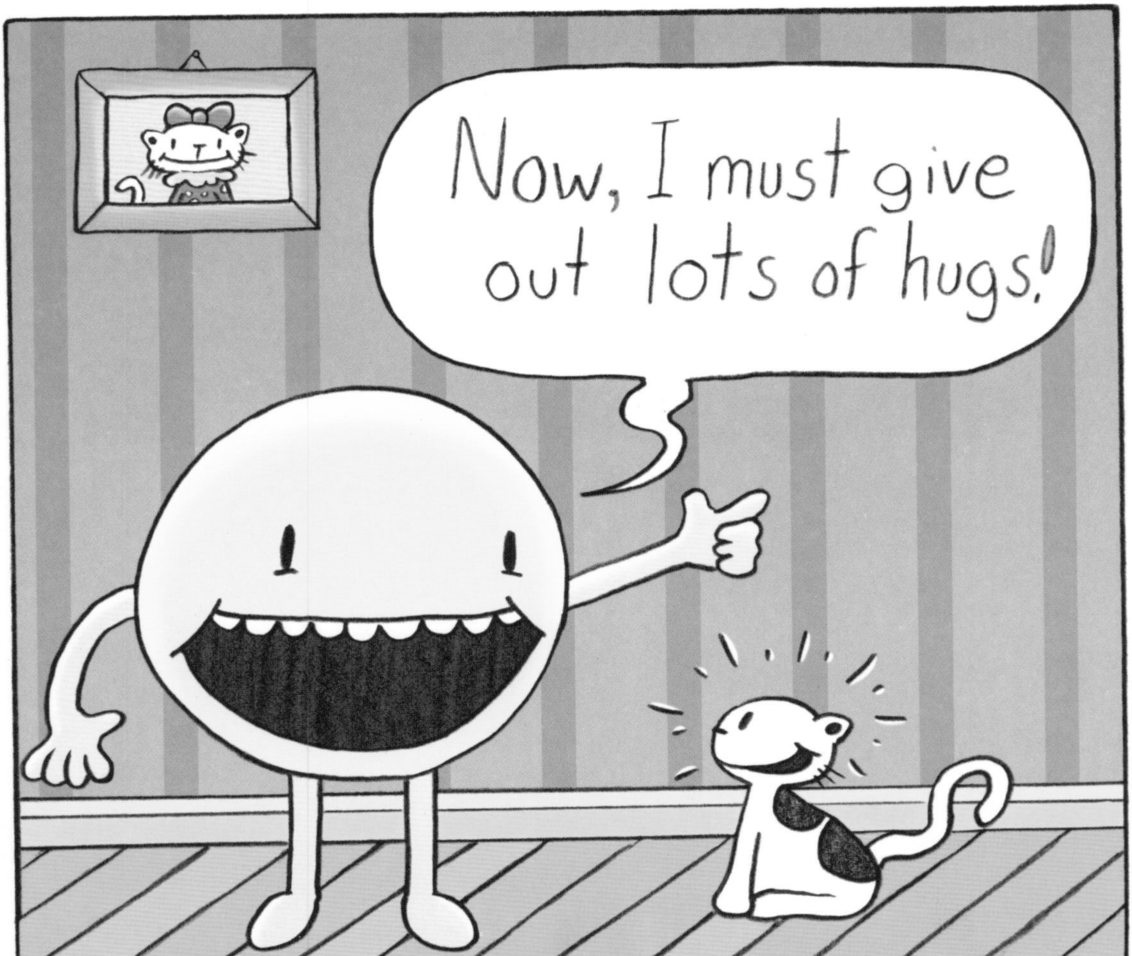
Now, I must give out lots of hugs!

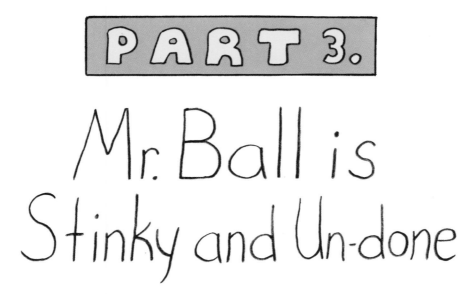

PART 3.

Mr. Ball is Stinky and Un-done

PART 4.

Mr. Ball does it ALL!!!

Join us next time when Mr. Ball baby sits some cute little sheep.

Just kidding!

But join us next time anyway, because...

THIS BOOK ENDS HERE